I0829399

Bob Mankoff's
Big Book
of
Relationship Cartoons

Featuring Cartoons From
Esquire
The New Yorker
& more!

All illustrations: Bob Mankoff
Book Design: Darren Kornblut

Cartoon Collections, LLC
10 Grand Central, 29th Floor
New York, NY 10017

For cartoon licensing information visit www.cartoonstock.com
Create a personalized version of this book at www.cartoonstockgifts.com

First edition published 2024

ISBN: 978-1-963079-06-7
Item # 47628

Introduction

This book is proof that you can judge a book by its cover.

Bob Mankoff's Big Book of Relationship Cartoons is exactly that, and I should know.

I've packed it with my best cartoons on dating, relationships, and marriage, that great trinity of our personal lives that evokes our deepest emotions and truest laughter.

This book doesn't shy away from the awkward moments of first dates or the silent standoffs of a fifty-year marriage. Instead, it embraces the folly that is love.

These cartoons remind us that even if we can't always make sense of relationships, we can at least find solace in knowing that we're not alone in our befuddlement.

After all, if you can't laugh at the existential rom-com that is human intimacy, then the joke's on you.

"*Sweetheart, I don't want anyone to make you unhappy except me.*"

"You look great. One problem though: I'm the one who goes to work."

"Gee, I thought you'd be happy to be the presumptive front-runner."

"Brad, we've got to talk."

"What do you say we let the service sector handle our dining needs for tonight?"

"So I says to your husband, 'Mr. Blanchard, go home to your wife.'
To which he retorts, 'You go home to her.' Ergo my presence."

"I don't mean to stir anything up, dear, but don't you think that perhaps our divorce was a little too amicable?"

"*There's nothing wrong with our marriage, but the spectre of gay marriage has hopelessly eroded the institution.*"

"Well, so long, Bert."

"It may surprise you to know that, contrary to your experience,
you're actually very happily married."

"*In case you're interested, I'll be in the basement preserving resentments for the winter.*"

"Hold that thought—I've just got two chapters to go."

"Look, there is no right and wrong here, but I'm going to side with Helen because I'm a girl."

"I'd like to say something to you, Miriam—strictly off the record, of course."

THE HOLE IN
THE OZONE
THE DESTRUCTION
OF THE
RAIN FOREST
MANKOFF
DIVISION OF LABOR

"*O.K., but what's our exit strategy?*"

TWO-THIRDS APPROVAL RATING

"Trust me, David, he meant nothing—it was just a training marriage."

"Amazing, eh? Good-looking, dependable, trustworthy, inflatable."

"Gee, Jeffrey, an annual report on our marriage is a novel anniversary gift,
but I was hoping for something a little more romantic."

"Well—and I'm not just saying this because you're my husband—it stinks."

"It's O.K., hon, it happens. It even happened to NATO."

"*Dear, what would you say to the idea of bringing more ethnic and gender diversity into our marriage?*"

"Hi. You've been randomly selected to participate in a
sex survey upstairs in fifteen minutes."

"Can I trouble you for a sexual favor?"

"*I love you, but not in that way.*"

"As a matter of fact, you did catch us at a bad time."

"Why won't you cuddle?"

"Ken bats left-handed, enjoys cultural as well as outdoor activities, and seeks a sensitive non-smoking woman for a lasting partnership that includes long walks, good music, and fielding practice."

"*What do you want Denise? I'm not a mind reader.*"

"Wow, I never realized your unhappiness was so nuanced."

"*Look, I can't promise I'll change, but I can promise I'll pretend to change.*"

"*No, Thursday's out. How about never—is never good for you?*"

"I have no idea our marriage was so interest-rate sensitive."

"*Look, I know it's not perfect, but, by and large,
the jury system has worked very well for
our marriage.*"

"*Edgar, I'm thinking of downsizing our marriage.*"

"*You mean you're just going to throw 274 mortgage payments out the window?*"

*"Marry you? Why I wouldn't even vote to
let you into my co-op."*

"*Have you noticed how blatant sex
is everywhere in the culture but here?*"

"*Great graphics, Dave, but the answer is still no.*"

"*Quick! Hide! That may be my husband!*"

"I was surprised myself, but living apart, seeing other people, and having virtually nothing to do with each other actually has made our marriage stronger."

"Who said anything about marriage? What I'm offering is an array of mutual funds, variable annuities and life insurance."

"That's my late husband."

MEN!
YOU CAN'T LIVE WITH 'EM, YOU CAN'T...
HEY, WAIT A MINUTE!
MANKOFF

"*OK, let's go to contract.*"

"Good news, hon—I've sold the ancillary rights to our marriage."

"Gee, Dave, a proposal to balance the budget wasn't really what I was expecting."

"And these two are from my first mortgage."

"Won't you please just look? It's not just a special advertising section – it's a very special advertising section."

"*Look, all I'm asking is that we let market forces bring a greater degree of efficiency into our marriage.*"

"Know what I think?
Of course."

"I'm sorry, dear. I wasn't listening.
Could you repeat what you've said since we've been married?"

"Mind if I put on the game?"

"*O.K., leave me, but just remember, if you do I'm coming with you.*"

"*Look, I'm quite sure you're mistaken—I never forget a spouse.*"

"It's amazing. We've just met, but I feel like we've known each other since we were kids, became high school sweethearts, got married too young, had a bunch of brats, went through a messy divorce, reconciled, remarried each other, and are now back together after all these years."

"Please, Dianna, at least give me a chance to rebrand myself."

*"What happened to us, Eddie? We used to be
so goal-oriented."*

"*Don't you think we should wait to see the effects of the new tax code?*"

"*Read your paper, dear. The news is getting cold.*"

"*See, it's right here in the pre-nup, Louise; if you walk out,*
I get two week severance sex."

"*Well, then, how about staying together for the sake of our joint checking account?*"

"*I think we're separated, but he says we just haven't seen each other in three years due to scheduling conflicts.*"

"*That was very nice, dear, but don't you think you should begin to address yourself to a broader constituency?*"

"I think you two may hit it off. Craig, here, is an attractive male academic in his early forties who seeks a warm, vivacious woman delighting in conversation, arts, and nature for an evolving romantic commitment, possibly marriage, while you, Vivian, are a good-looking, intelligent, stimulating woman in her late thirties who seeks an educated, unattached, well-bred man concerned with ideas, culture, and the environment with whom to share your life interests and companionship."

"*You know, lately I've been fantasizing about having a twosome.*"

"Hey, I'm in the mood for love—be back in a few hours."

"Great PowerPoint, Kevin, but the answer is no."

"Y'know, I don't know what I'd do without her, but I'd sure like to find out."

"Hi. We're grass-roots ad-hoc committee to save
your marriage. May we come in?"

"*What do you mean, 'Marriage is a two-edged sword'?*"

"*I'm sorry, Dave, but our marriage has lost its narrative flow.*"

*"Dear, I'd like you to meet the Donaldsons
and their model marriage."*

"*And this one is for being faithful to my wife.*"

"*This is my last visit, Martha. I got the marriage posthumously annulled.*"

"*No, I don't think our marriage would benefit from a mission statement.*"

"Believe me, Janet, I consider you an important part of our marriage."

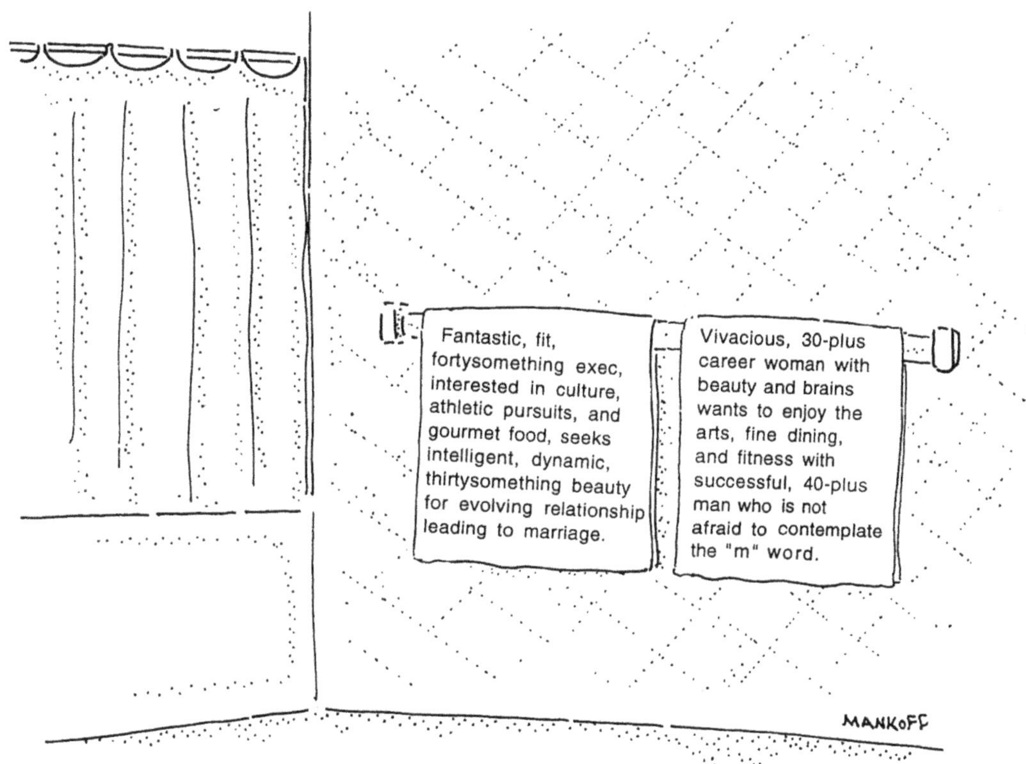

Fantastic, fit, fortysomething exec, interested in culture, athletic pursuits, and gourmet food, seeks intelligent, dynamic, thirtysomething beauty for evolving relationship leading to marriage.
Vivacious, 30-plus career woman with beauty and brains wants to enjoy the arts, fine dining, and fitness with successful, 40-plus man who is not afraid to contemplate the "m" word.
MANKOFF

"So, how's your snit coming?"

"Diane, this is Karen, an old war buddy of mine."

"*Can I have another piece of the paper?*"

"But what about all our refinancing plans?"

"*Look, hon, I know both of our schedules have been crazy, but I still think we should take time out to consummate our marriage.*"

"Why, you're right. Tonight isn't reading night, tonight is sex night."

*"Oh, there's nothing really wrong with our marriage.
We'd just like to figure out a way to monetize it."*

"I don't want to sound simplistic, but I think a smaller couch with fewer throw pillows would help this marriage a lot."

"No, he didn't suffer. That's my only regret."

"*But that was the old me—this is the remix.*"

"Quick! Hide! That may be my husband!"

"In the mood for a little sexual misconduct?"

FOR
SALE

MANKOFF

"Dear, did something happen at the office?"

"*Don't take it personally, Dan,
it's just a career move.*"

"*Hon, this is Mr Atherton. He's going to show us how we can commercially exploit our marriage.*"

"As long as you're going out, how about hustling up a few bucks."

"You'll be back."

*"A No-Nonsense Guy with His No-Nonsense Wife
and Their No-Nonsense Dog"*

"None for me, thanks."

"Interesting. Have your lawyer call my lawyer."

"*I don't know about you, but I'm ready to take this marriage full-throttle.*"

*"Look, I can deal with a sexless marriage, but,
for God's sake, we're having an affair!"*

"Might I sound a note of caution?"

MINIMUM—SECURITY PRISON
MANKOFF

"See, it's right here in the pre-nup. If you walk out, I get two weeks' severance sex."

"So soon? But we've barely scratched the surface of our discontent."

"*I had a nice time, Steve. Would you like to come in, settle down, and raise a family?*"

"*Now that the kids are grown and gone, I thought it might be a good time for us to have sex.*"

"Maybe you ought to consider making love in the morning—before you have a chance to piss each other off."

"We're in love."   "Details at eleven."

"*This doesn't have anything to do with the falling price of oil, does it?*"

"*Oh, I guess I'll remarry someday. But first I've got to demarry.*"

"This is Dave, my friend plus."

DAVE AND HIS COMMON-LAW ACCOUNTANT, PHIL

"And, for music, you want traditional
or new age?"

"*Could I have some privacy? It's my boyfriend.*"

"Well, Bob, bed wasn't much, but, I must say, breakfast is delicious."

*"Well, Elaine, it looks as though we're not on the
same page when it comes to the fidelity issue."*

WORKING MARRIAGE
MANKOFF

"We're pretty traditional around here. I handle everything on the domestic front except security."

"*Advantage, Mom.*"

"*Women want more these days, Bill—it's not enough just to be a jerk anymore.*"

"Well, what you call an affair I prefer to call an anomaly."

"*Amazing! Our first date and I feel we've known each other all our lives.*"

"For God's sake, Edith, I'm trying to read the paper!"

"Edgar, I think it's time we told my husband about us."

128

"*Dave, could you hold on a sec while I take care of some personal business?*"

"Let's do it, let's fall in love."

"*What do you mean, you're getting cold feet?*
We've been married six years."

"*Don't be silly—we're being perfectly fine hosts.*"

"Gee, Dave, a proposal to balance the budget wasn't really what I was expecting."

"Look, you've been great. It's just that we'd like to start seeing other marriage counsellors."

"I've lost track. Are you unhappy because I said you were making me unhappy or is it the other way around?"

"*And this is my late husband.*"

"By the way, what's your position on some-sex marriage?"

"Happy Valentine's day!"

"Hey! How about giving me some benchmarks?"

"True, you have irreconcilable differences, but they're mainly about flossing."

"I know it's not perfect, but, by and large, I think the jury system has served this marriage very well."

"Hey! Can't a guy have a hobby?"

"*Oh, nothing. I was just hoping our affair would be more sordid.*"

"*You're a good husband, Dave—I just want to start marrying other people.*"

"*Believe me, it's not what it is.*"

"*Silly man, that wasn't an affair—I was just riffing on our marriage.*"

About Bob Mankoff

For over 40 years, Bob Mankoff has been the driving force of comedy and satire at some of the most honored publications in America, including *The New Yorker* and *Esquire.* He has devoted his life to discovering what makes us laugh and seeks every outlet to do so, from developing *The New Yorker*'s web presence to integrating it with algorithms and AI. Mankoff is currently the cartoon editor at the weekly online newsletter *Air Mail.*

A student of humor and creativity, Mankoff has taught classes on
The Psychology of Humor at The University of Michigan, Swarthmore, Fordham, and has led workshops on the creative process.

In 2018, Mankoff launched CartoonStock.com, a new spin on the Cartoon Bank, the world's most successful cartoon licensing platform he founded in 1992. At Cartoon Collections, Bob has brought together cartoons from the *New Yorker* and previously unavailable cartoons from *National Lampoon, Esquire, Wall Street Journal,* and *Barron*'s to create the world's largest cartoon licensing source.